Give your child a head start with
PICTURE READERS

Dear Parent,

Now children as young as preschool age can have the fun and satisfaction of reading a book all on their own.

In every Picture Reader, there are simple words, rebus pictures, and 24 flash cards to cut out and keep. (There is a flash card for every rebus picture plus extra cards for reading practice.) After children listen to each story a couple of times, they will be ready to try it all by themselves.

Collect all the titles in our Picture Reader series. Once children have mastered these books, they can move on to Levels 1, 2, and 3 in our All Aboard Reading series.

For my dear father-in-law,
Dr. Edward F. Lewison, with warm wishes
for many happy, snowy days—W.C.L.

To the snow-loving children of the Clark and
Wilkins Elementary Schools, Amherst, N.H.
Warm wishes—M.C-L.

ISBN 0-439-37532-0

12 11 10   4 5 6/0

Printed in the U.S.A.   23

First Scholastic printing, November 2001

A PICTURE READER

The BIG SNOWBALL

By Wendy Cheyette Lewison
Illustrated by Maryann Cocca-Leffler

SCHOLASTIC INC.

New York Toronto London Auckland Sydney
Mexico City New Delhi Hong Kong Buenos Aires

Up on a

that was very tall,

a little

made a big .

He gave that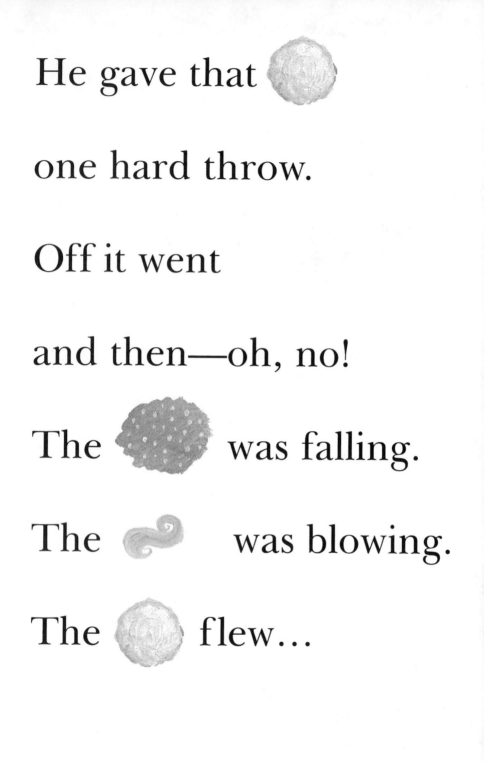

one hard throw.

Off it went

and then—oh, no!

The was falling.

The was blowing.

The flew...

and kept on going!

It went past and

 on .

It went over

everybody's .

It stopped the .

It stopped the .

It scared the

off some .

It chased away

a and a .

It knocked off

many people's .

But still the

did not stop.

It flew into

the ice-cream shop.

And while Miss Jones

was on the ,

it dropped into

an ice-cream .

Just then, the

came in, of course.

He was as hungry

as a .

He wanted something

good to eat...

so with a

he bought a treat.

That's all.

No more !

boy	hill
snow	snowball
boys	wind

sleds	girls
cars	heads
feathers	trucks

dog	ducks
hats	cat
cone	phone

dollar	horse
scarf	mittens
tree	boots